THE ORIGIN OF
Bonsai

The word bonsai is derived from two Japanese words: "bon" meaning tray or dish, and "sai" meaning tree or plant. Thus, a bonsai is a tree or shrub grown in a container.

Although usually thought of as Japanese, the art of bonsai began in China more than 2000 years ago. During the tenth or eleventh century, bonsai was brought to Japan by Buddhist monks. At first, people hunted for dwarf trees that had been confined by rocks and formed by wind and erosion. Later, artists began to copy nature by pruning the roots and shaping branches with special tools.

Once honored as religious objects, bonsai trees are now seen as living sculpture. Unlike paintings or statues, they continue to grow and may live more than 100 years.

🐸 🐸 🐸

To Marian, for everything.
Bernie Libster

To all the parents who love their children as they are.
Aries Cheung

The Bonsai Bear

By Bernard Libster

Illustrations by Aries Cheung

ILLUMINATION
Arts

PUBLISHING COMPANY, INC.
BELLEVUE, WASHINGTON

Many years ago, in a remote Japanese village, there lived a childless couple.

Kyomi, the wife, knew many wonderful things. She made paper birds that looked ready to fly from her hand, and paper flowers that seemed to fill the air with a fragrant perfume. She painted mountains that echoed with the wind, and rivers that left onlookers feeling splashed with water. Into her exquisite cloth she wove beautiful patterns using strands of her long black hair.

Kyomi's husband, Issa, knew only one thing well, but this he knew better than anyone in all of Japan. He was the supreme master of bonsai. With a few snips of his scissors and twists of fine wire applied in secret places, Issa could make trees stay whatever size and shape he chose – even trees whose nature it was to grow wild and grand.

Issa took such great pride in his little bonsai trees, they gave every appearance of knowing they were masterpieces.

Every day Kyomi and Issa walked in the mountains. Kyomi rejoiced in all she saw and heard – the sunlight sparkling on the water, the sound of rushing rivers. She loved the birds soaring high in the sky and the trees that grew so tall they seemed to hold up the clouds.

Issa also loved the mountains, but always his restless eyes
searched the crags for young trees that he could transform into his
beloved bonsai.

Slowly a strange desire grew within Issa's heart. "If I could create a bonsai that walks about yet remains as small and perfect as my trees," he said to himself, "I would be the greatest bonsai master who ever lived."

One night Issa dreamed of holding a small animal in his arms. For a time he simply stroked its fur. Then he picked up his scissors and began to snip furiously. As the little creature looked up at him with trusting brown eyes, a stern voice interrupted Issa's dream. "An animal is not a tree. You must find another way."

When he awoke, Issa remembered only the trusting eyes.

The very next morning, Kyomi and Issa heard a knock at the door. There stood their friend Basho, who carried in his cloak a small bundle – a bundle that began to wriggle.

"What have you here?" Kyomi asked. "Is it a puppy?"

The wily Basho shook his head.

"It is a kitten!" exclaimed Issa.

Basho smiled and opened his cloak.

"Why, it's a bear!" the amazed couple exclaimed. "Wherever did you find him?"

"I was walking in the woods," said Basho, "when I came upon a lifeless mother bear. This pathetic little fellow lay curled up against her, crying his eyes out. You are good at caring for things," Basho continued. "Perhaps you will keep him until he can look after himself."

"The Emperor forbids keeping wild creatures," said Issa, who did not wish to be sent to prison. But he could not take his eyes off the tiny bear, who fell peacefully asleep as Kyomi held him gently to her breast.

And so the bear stayed with Kyomi and Issa,
who quickly came to love him.

Unfortunately the little fellow was growing so fast that it
would soon be impossible to hide him from visitors, who might
inform the Emperor. Even so, they could not imagine parting with
their extraordinary pet.

The day came when Issa could resist no longer. Taking the tiny animal in his arms, he reached for his scissors. But as the bear's soft breath touched his cheek, Issa remembered the voice, the voice that said, "You must find another way."

Issa put down his scissors. Suddenly he knew what to do. "I will bind him," he whispered to himself, "with something that Kyomi will never notice, something so strong and so delicate that his skin will not be cut."

Issa went to Kyomi's dressing table and took from her brush several strands of her long, black hair. After carefully binding the bear in secret places, he hurried away before Kyomi returned.

From then on, the bear stopped growing. With a few snips of his scissors, Issa would trim the bear's fur just as he would shape a bonsai tree. Every so often, he secretly took a few more strands of Kyomi's hair to bind the little creature.

One day, Issa could no longer contain his pride. "Our bear can stay with us forever now," he told Kyomi. "I have made him into a bonsai."

Kyomi stood silently for a very long time. At last she spoke. "This is shameful, my husband. Big or small, trees are content to stay in one place. But bears must run freely wherever they desire."

"Our bear *can* run freely," Issa replied. "Just see how he frolics with us."

"Bears belong in the forest," Kyomi declared. "They must climb over great boulders and swim mighty rivers. Our bear cannot do this when he is so small."

Issa knew that Kyomi was right, but his heart remained filled with pride. "You want him to grow and leave us!" he shouted angrily.

Issa's words hurt Kyomi. Instead of painting and weaving she spent many hours singing sadly to herself. She hoped her husband's heart would change.

The little bear sensed that he had brought great sorrow into the lives of his friends. He wanted so much to make them happy that he began to romp about doing silly things, the way a clown does. The grateful Issa named him Doukeshi, an ancient word meaning "jester," one who lightens hearts. "Doukeshi," Issa said softly, "my bonsai bear."

One day Issa had an inspiration. He cut a branch from a rare and precious bonsai whose thick brown needles were exactly the color of Doukeshi's coat. From the branch, he fashioned a long tail and a pair of pointed ears, which he skillfully attached to the little bear. Doukeshi now looked just like a cat.

Friends who came to visit marveled at the adorable little creature with his wonderful sweetness of nature. Doukeshi even learned to purr almost like a real cat. No one noticed that he was really a bear, so no one reported to the Emperor.

19

Doukeshi might soon have forgotten his true nature, but Kyomi did not forget.

Every night, after Issa was asleep, she held the little creature and sang to him. "You are a bear and you must never forget who you are. One day you will be free. As you run through the forest and swim great rivers, my heart will always be with you."

Kyomi's song stirred the little bear. He remembered the smell of the den where he was born, the comfort of his mother's warmth, and the taste of her milk. Poor Doukeshi felt torn apart. Issa wanted him to stay small forever. Kyomi wanted him to grow. What would become of him?

One night the God of Bears came into Doukeshi's dream with a great roar, "Prepare to live in the forest," he commanded. "You will soon be a mighty bear!"

Now Doukeshi, in the way of animals, knew patience. He remained content to walk under Issa's hand and be petted, and to snuggle close to Kyomi and feel her heart beat. Yet at night, rivers roared through his dreams, and he tasted salmon and wild berries. In the morning he would wake as a cat, but at night he dreamed as a bear.

As Issa slept one night, his soul was touched by the soul of his little bear. Issa, too, heard the howl of fierce winds and watched little creatures scurry away as the mighty Doukeshi charged through the forest.

In his heart Issa had become one with his beloved pet. But still, he could not lift a finger to undo his art.

The following night, the God of Bears appeared in Issa's dream. In one gigantic paw, he snatched up the dreaming Issa and, with razor-sharp teeth, went snip snip in secret places. And Issa became a tiny bonsai man.

Issa awoke shivering. "I must free Doukeshi," he whispered.

Kyomi's heart leapt with joy. "Can you do this?" she asked. "He has been a bonsai for so long."

"I must try," Isssa answered. "A tree is a tree, and a bear must be allowed to be a bear." He rose from his bed and gathered Doukeshi in his arms. First he removed the cat ears and tail. Then he cut the strands of hair and brought the little bear's face close to his. "Forgive me," he whispered, "for what I have done to you."

From that day on, Doukeshi slept more and more. As he dreamed, the God of Bears taught him how to live in the forest – to sense prey behind rocks and trees – to make a den for the long winter – and to be wary of the scent of man, who is often his enemy and rarely, like Kyomi and Issa, his friend.

Doukeshi quickly grew too big for his bed, too big even for Issa and Kyomi's bed. Every night as Kyomi stroked his thick fur, she sang a joyful song mixed with sadness. She knew that this creature she loved so dearly soon would be gone forever.

One day in autumn it was done. He who had been a bonsai now stood a fully grown bear who would soon face the winter alone. Doukeshi understood that when winter was over, he would emerge from his den and live as a bear – a bear who could race swiftly through the mountains and snatch fish from icy rivers. He felt a pride he had never known before.

When Kyomi and Issa opened the door to their home that special morning, Doukeshi could barely pass through. For the last time, he walked under Issa's hand and snuggled so close to Kyomi he could feel her heart beat.

But now he must know love in other ways. Doukeshi turned his great brown eyes to Kyomi and Issa. They shivered as a spark of his soul flowed into their hearts.

Then he was gone, gone forever into the forest and to the God of Bears.

Issa returned in peace to his bonsai. Each time he lovingly fashioned a little tree, he remembered his departed pet. One spring day as his wife sat painting a sky full of soaring birds, Issa said, "Kyomi, we must find another pet to keep us company."

"Yes, that is a fine idea," she said, "and I know just what to name him."

ILLUMINATION Arts

PUBLISHING COMPANY, INC.

P.O. Box 1865, Bellevue, WA 98009
Tel: 425-644-7185 ✧ 888-210-8216 (orders only) ✧ Fax: 425-644-9274
liteinfo@illumin.com ✧ http://www.illumin.com

Library of Congress Cataloging-in-Publication Data

Libster, Bernard, 1940-
 The bonsai bear / by Bernard Libster ; illustrations by Aries Cheung.
   p. cm.
 Summary: A Japanese artist uses bonsai cultivating techniques to control and limit the growth of a young bear, not caring that he is denying the animal his proper place in nature.
 ISBN 0-935699-15-5
 [1. Bears—Fiction. 2. Bonsai—Fiction. 3. Animals—Treatment—Fiction. 4. Japan—Fiction.] I. Cheung, Aries, 1960- ill. II. Title.
 PZ7.L59123Bo 1999   98-42666
                                                             CIP
                                                             AC

Published in the United States of America
Printed by Star Standard Industries in Singapore

Book Designer:
Molly Murrah, Murrah & Company, Kirkland, WA

Illumination Arts' Children's Books Are Available at Fine Bookstores Everywhere

TO SLEEP WITH THE ANGELS

By H. Elizabeth Collins, illustrated by Judy Kuusisto $15.95, 0-935699-16-3

Every night, a young girl is taken by her guardian angel on inspiring adventures. Angels of many races are pictured in this special book, sure to become a nighttime "read-again" tradition. Ages 3 to adult.

DRAGON

Written and illustrated by Jody Bergsma $15.95, 0-935699-17-1

Born on the same day, a gentle prince and a firebreathing dragon share a prophetic destiny before the prince can become king. Ages 6 to adult.

SKY CASTLE

By Sandra Hanken, illustrated by Jody Bergsma $15.95, 0-935699-14-7

Selected as a "Children's Choice for 1999" by Children's Book Council

High above the clouds, three charming fairies help us create a majestic castle for all the world's creatures. This colorful Celtic tale, alive with winged dragons and teddy bears, inspires children of all ages to believe in the power of dreams. Ages 3 to adult.

DREAMBIRDS

By David Ogden, illustrated by Jody Bergsma $16.95, 0-935699-09-0

1998 Visionary Award for Best Children's Book – Coalition of Visionary Retailers

The magical story of a Native American boy's search for the gift of the illusive dreambird. The spectacular illustrations of Northwest wildlife "exceed the highest standards for the genre." – Birdwatchers Digest. Ages 5 to adult.

THE RIGHT TOUCH

A Read-Aloud Story to Help Prevent Child Sexual Abuse

By Sandy Kleven, LCSW; illustrated by Jody Bergsma $15.95, 0-935699-10-4

Winner – 1999 Benjamin Franklin Award

Young Jimmy's mother gently explains how he can protect himself from improper touching. Selected as Outstanding by the Parents Council,® this book is suitable for children as young as age 3.

ALL I SEE IS PART OF ME

By Chara M. Curtis, illustrated by Cynthia Aldrich $15.95, 0-935699-07-4

Winner – 1996 Award of Excellence from Body Mind Spirit Magazine

This inspirational classic appeals to all ages. A child discovers his common link with the Universe. Inspired by Sister Star, he feels the light within his heart and then finds that same light in all others. Readers' hearts are deeply touched. Ages 2 to adult.

FUN IS A FEELING

By Chara M. Curtis, illustrated by Cynthia Aldrich $15.95, 0-935699-13-9

Refreshing rhymes and inspiring illustrations encourage readers to discover the fun hidden in all of life's experiences. "Fun isn't something or somewhere or who. It's a feeling of joy that lives inside of you." Ages 3 to adult.

HOW FAR TO HEAVEN?

By Chara M. Curtis, illustrated by Alfred Currier $15.95, 0-935699-06-6

Nanna and her granddaughter explore the wonders of nature to discover how close heaven really is. A magnificently illustrated favorite with nature-lovers and those who have lost a loved one. Ages 4 to adult.

CORNELIUS AND THE DOG STAR

By Diana Spyropulos, illustrated by Ray Williams $15.95, 0-935699-08-2

Winner – 1996 Award of Excellence from Body Mind Spirit Magazine

After grouchy old Cornelius Basset-Hound takes his last breath, he is swept directly to the gates of Dog Heaven. His amazing adventure begins when Saint Bernard says he must learn about love, generosity, and playfulness. Ages 4 to adult.

ILLUMINATION ARTS PUBLISHING COMPANY

P.O. Box 1865, Bellevue, WA 98009

Tel: 425-644-7185 ❧ 888-210-8216 ❧ Fax: 425-644-9274

liteinfo@illumin.com ❧ http://www.illumin.com

Direct U.S. orders: Add $2.00 for postage; each additional book, add $1.00;
Washington residents, add 8.6% state sales tax.